Digital Monster Madness

Modern Publishing
A Division of Unisystems, Inc.
New York, New York 10022

Printed in the U.S.A.
Series UPC #19335

86-23760

Summer camp was supposed to be a really great way to spend summer vacation. It might have been if we were there longer.

One minute the seven of us were just enjoying ourselves, the next, we were sailing through space on our way to a strange new world where creatures called Digimon—digital monsters—live.

MOTIMON

TOKOMON

TANEMON

Things got completely unreal when these digital monsters digivolved into even cooler digital monsters.

TENTOMON

PATAMON

PALMON

TSUNOMON

YOKOMON

BUKAMON

KOROMON

There was one for each of us and they had incredible powers.

GABUMON

BIYOMON

GOMAMON

AGUMON

Then they fought off this giant evil digital monster bug that wanted us for a meal. If our Digimons hadn't been able to digivolve, we'd be digibug food by now. Kuwagamon sure looked tough . . .

But he didn't stand a chance against Agumon and the gang. The digital monsters really saved our lives.

DigiWorld would be a great place to live if we didn't have to run for our lives all the time.

Having to fight off Shellmon so soon after defeating Kuwagamon sure put a strain on our Digimons.

Shellmon grabbed Tai in his hair. Talk about having a bad hair day. Agumon tried to save Tai with his pepper breath. But it had no effect on Shellmon.

Then Agumon digivolved into Greymon and really let Shellmon have it.

Later we learned that our Digimons digivolve into champions when any of us are in really great danger. DigiWorld is loaded with danger. And that's why we should be extra careful. There are some big, scary monsters out there who want to eat people like me and T.K.

I'm not afraid. I wasn't afraid when we saw those Monochromon either. Even though they didn't bother us, we all agreed running away was a good idea.

After we left the Monochromon behind, we needed a place to rest for the night. We were lucky to find that abandoned train car.

I took the first watch that night. And it was a good thing someone did. Otherwise we would not have known that Seadramon was about to attack.

Seadramon's serpent attack was so sudden. Matt was trapped in Seadramon's tail. To save Matt, Gabumon digivolved into the giant wolf-like Garurumon.

Then Garurumon gave
Seadramon a serious thrashing.

Sometime later, after drying off Matt, we found a small village inhabited by Yokomons.

The Yokomons told us about a Digimon that lived in the nearby volcano. They said the fiery Meramon wasn't usually violent but something had changed him. Biyomon digivolved into Birdramon and fought Meramon when he came down from his volcanic mountain.

Birdramon's attack knocked a mysterious Black Gear out of Meramon. As soon as the gear was gone and the battle was over, Meramon told the Yokomons and us that he was really sorry for causing so much trouble.

From then on, we kept a sharp eye out for the mysterious Black Gear as we went along.

Even the child-loving guardian of toys, Monzaemon, attacked us because of a Black Gear.

Our Digimons got us
out of that mess too.

But right now, all we need to do is find our way home as quickly as we can. Who knows what we'll face next? As long as we have our Digimons by our sides, we'll be all right.